little bee books

251 Park Avenue South, New York, NY 10010
Copyright © 2017 by Little Bee Books
All rights reserved, including the right of reproduction
in whole or in part in any form.
Manufactured in the United States of America LB 0719
ISBN: 978-1-4998-0390-7 (hc)
First Edition 10 9 8 7 6 5 4 3 2
ISBN: 978-1-4998-0389-1 (pbk)
First Edition 10 9 8 7 6 5 4

Names: Pearl, Alexa, 1967- author. | Sordo, Paco, illustrator.
Title: Big secret / by Alexa Pearl ; illustrated by Paco Sordo.
Description: New York, New York : Little Bee Books, [2017] | Series: Tales of Sasha; #1 |
Summary: "In the Tales of Sasha series debut, Sasha discovers that she really isn't like the other horses in her valley when wings sprout from her back and she soars through the air!"—Provided by publisher.
Identifiers: LCCN 2016004446| ISBN 9781499803891 (pbk) | ISBN 9781499803907 (hc)
Subjects: | CYAC: Horses—Fiction. | Animals, Mythical—Fiction. | Identity—Fiction. | Secrets—Fiction. | BISAC: JUVENILE FICTION / Readers / Chapter Books. | JUVENILE FICTION / Animals / Horses. | JUVENILE FICTION / Animals / Mythical.
Classification: LCC PZ7.1.P425 Bi 2016 | DDC [Fic]—dc23
LC record available at https://lccn.loc.gov/2016004446

littlebeebooks.com

Tales of
SASHA

The Big
Secret

by Alexa Pearl
illustrated by Paco Sordo

little bee books

Contents

Go! Go! Go!

"Sasha! Come back!"

Sasha's ears perked up, but she did not stop running. She was having too much fun. She ran past her friends. She ran past her two sisters. Faster and faster. The wind flowed through her glossy mane. The sun felt warm on her back. The spring grass was bright green beneath her hooves.

Up ahead, she spotted the stream. She did not slow down. She ran toward it.

One . . . two . . . *three!* Sasha counted to herself. Then she leaped into the air. Her body felt so light it was like she was floating in the clouds. *This is the best feeling EVER!* she thought.

Sasha landed on the
other side of the stream.
A forest of tall trees
stood in front of her.

"Sasha! Come back!"

Her mom's voice stopped her. Sasha knew that tone. That tone meant her mom was upset, and Sasha knew why. The horses in their valley all had the same rule: Never go beyond the big trees.

Now she was standing in front of the big trees. She had never run this far before.

What is beyond the trees? she wondered.

No one in Verdant Valley knew. Not Mom. Not Dad. Not her teacher. Not her sisters.

I hate not knowing things, Sasha thought. *Someday I will go there. Someday I will find out.*

Sasha splashed back through the stream. She trotted to her family.

Her mom frowned. "I warned you not to run too far, Sasha," she said.

"I'm sorry," said Sasha.

Mom nuzzled her with her nose. Sasha nuzzled back. Sasha's mom never stayed angry with her.

"Was someone chasing you?" asked her sister Zara. Zara was the oldest sister in their family. Poppy was in the middle, and Sasha was the youngest.

Sasha laughed. "No. Why?"

"You were running so fast," said Zara.

"Running makes me tired and sweaty," said Poppy.

Running makes me super happy, Sasha thought.

She had once tried to tell her sisters about how great she felt when she ran. They did not understand. They liked to spend their days eating grass and talking. Sasha thought that was boring.

Zara and Poppy were so different from Sasha. They looked different too.

Zara was jet-black with a chestnut brown mane and tail. Poppy was chestnut brown with a jet-black mane and tail. Their dad called them the "flip-flop sisters." Everyone could see that they belonged together.

And then there was Sasha. She was pale gray—except for a small white patch on her back. Her tail and mane were gray too. *Borrrring!* thought Sasha.

Whenever she ran, Sasha pretended that she was shiny silver. She pretended that her mane glittered. She even pretended that rainbow sparkles exploded from her tail.

Sasha wished she looked as sparkly as she felt. She wished she could be a "flip-flop sister" too.

"I'm putting flowers in Zara's mane," said Poppy.

"Do you want flowers in yours?" asked Zara.

"Yes!" said Sasha. "We can *all* wear pretty flowers."

Poppy tucked a flower into Sasha's mane, but it fell out. Poppy put in another flower, but that one fell out too.

"Sasha!" cried Poppy. "Stay still. The flowers are falling."

I stink at staying still, thought Sasha, but she tried to be like her sisters. She tried not to move. Then her hooves did a little dance. Her body wanted to go, go, go!

Wyatt trotted over. Wyatt was Sasha's better-than-best friend. He swatted her with his tail.

"Tag! You're it!" cried Wyatt.

Sasha was off! She chased after Wyatt. All the flowers fell out, but Sasha did not care.

Wyatt was fast, but Sasha was faster!

Head in the Clouds

"Got you!" Sasha tagged Wyatt.

"Let's play again," said Wyatt. "This time you won't catch me."

"Sure!" But Sasha knew she would catch him. She always did.

A loud whinny echoed through the valley. The whinny sounded again. Caleb, their teacher, was calling them.

"It's time for school," said Wyatt.

Caleb waited in the shade of a pine tree. All the young horses trotted over to him. Zara and Poppy galloped up. Sasha and Wyatt went too.

Caleb was the oldest horse in their valley. There were flecks of gray in his copper coat. He had taught Sasha's parents when they were young. Caleb was very smart. He knew everything about everything.

"Today, we will learn to walk in a line." Caleb spoke very slowly.

"But why?" asked Twinkle. Twinkle was always asking questions.

"Horses walk in a line to go to the pasture to eat," said Caleb. Caleb showed them how.

Sasha yawned. Caleb walked as slowly as he talked.

All the horses watched Caleb—except Sasha. She watched a butterfly flutter up and down. She watched a bumblebee buzz over a purple flower. She watched a red-tailed hawk soar through the sky. Her heart beat in time to the beating of their wings.

She imagined the world from above. Did the air taste sweeter? What would their valley look like from high up in the clouds?

If I could fly, thought Sasha, *I would spread my wings like the hawk and fly to faraway places. . . .*

"Sasha? Sasha?" Caleb's voice broke through her thoughts. "What is the answer, Sasha?"

"Uh, well . . ." Sasha flattened her ears to her head. Her face grew hot. She didn't know the answer. She hadn't heard the question.

Caleb sighed. "Sasha has her head in the clouds again."

"What's that mean?" asked Twinkle. "Her head is right here on her body."

"That means Sasha was daydreaming," explained Caleb. "Sasha, eyes on me. Okay?"

"Okay," said Sasha. She tried to pay attention. She really did, but her skin itched—right by the white patch on her back. That itch made her want to move, run, and soar. She looked up at the sky. She wished her head really *were* in the clouds.

CHAPTER 3

The Big Sneeze

"Everyone, find a partner," Caleb told the class.

Hooves pounded as they all scrambled to pair up. Sasha hurried to Wyatt, but Chester was already at his side.

"I'm sorry, Sasha," said Wyatt. He and Chester were partners.

Zara and Poppy stood together. Sasha's sisters were partners.

Sasha turned to Twinkle. "Partners?"
Sasha asked hopefully.

Twinkle shook her head.

"No?" Sasha gulped. "Why not?"

"You don't listen. You get into trouble
a lot," said Twinkle.

"No, I don't—" started Sasha. Then she stopped. She *did* get into trouble a lot. She tried to tell Twinkle why. "Sometimes, I feel like I'm standing at the starting line of a race, waiting for the whistle to blow."

Twinkle wrinkled her nose. "What race? There's no race."

"I know." Sasha searched for the right words to make Twinkle understand. "I keep getting an itchy feeling that something exciting is about to happen. It makes me fidget. I can't pay attention. Then I get into trouble."

"I need a good partner," Twinkle told her. "I want to get a good grade."

"I'll listen. I promise," said Sasha. "Please, can we be partners?"

"Okay." Twinkle smiled, and her brown eyes twinkled. That was how she'd gotten her name.

"Partners need to walk nose to tail," Caleb told the class. "Choose who is in the front and who is in the back."

"I'll be in front," said Twinkle.

"I'll be in back," agreed Sasha.

"Both partners must stay in step with each other," said Caleb. "Walk together around the pine tree, around the log, and past the big, flat rock."

"That isn't hard," Sasha told Twinkle.

They set off. Sasha kept a close watch on Twinkle's hooves. She stepped at the same time that Twinkle stepped.

"Right, left, right," said Twinkle. They walked around the pine tree.

Swish! Twinkle's tail brushed Sasha's face. The long hair tickled her nose. *Ah-ah-ah . . .*

Oh no! Sasha felt a sneeze coming—a big sneeze.

I'll mess up if I sneeze, she thought. *I can't do that to Twinkle.*

Sasha tried to hold in her sneeze. She pushed her tongue against her teeth. She closed her mouth. Her eyes bulged. Her nose twitched.

Could she do it?

CHAPTER 4) Up in the Air

Sasha did it! The sneeze went away.

"Look at the cute turtles on the log!" Twinkle called back to her.

Sasha couldn't see the turtles. All she could see was Twinkle's backside, and she didn't want to see that! Sasha raised her head high and saw the hawk again. She watched him make lazy circles over the big trees.

"*Psst*, Twinkle," whispered Sasha. "What do you think is beyond the big trees?"

"More trees?" guessed Twinkle.

"I think there are huge, crunchy pink-and-purple fruits. They taste sour and sweet at the same time. I think there are tall flowers. And the flowers have faces. Funny faces," said Sasha. She made a funny face too.

"You're silly, Sasha," said Twinkle. Sasha didn't think so.

"I want to go there someday. Do you want to come with me?" asked Sasha.

"Nope." Twinkle kept walking.

"Why not?" asked Sasha.

"I'm happy here. My family is here. I don't want to go anywhere else," said Twinkle.

Sasha didn't understand. Couldn't Twinkle feel that something amazing waited beyond their valley? Something way more amazing than learning to walk in a line!

Sasha loved her family and her home, but she knew they'd always be waiting here. She dreamed of exploring.

"The flat rock is coming up," said Twinkle.

Sasha spotted the rock. The patch
on her back began to itch. She tried to
ignore it. "Right, left, right," Sasha said.

The patch kept itching. It made her
tail flick back and forth. It made her
hooves go *tap, tap, tap*.

"Twinkle," she said suddenly, "let's jump *over* the rock!"

"No way!" cried Twinkle. "We'll get in trouble."

"Come on! It'll be so much fun," said Sasha.

"You promised to be a good partner." Twinkle turned to look at Sasha. Her eyes were not twinkling anymore. "Go *around* the rock—not over."

"Around," agreed Sasha. She shook her head to shake away the feeling, but her body still wanted to soar over the rock. One big leap. Up, up, up.

No, she scolded herself. *Friends keep promises.* Sasha wanted to be a good friend—and a good partner. She stayed behind Twinkle. Then she couldn't help it. She stepped out of line.

"Sasha!" Twinkle exclaimed, as she twisted to look at Caleb. "Get back in line!"

Sasha's legs kept moving. Her white patch itched. The itching made her legs go faster. She trotted past Twinkle. Then she cantered by Caleb.

Caleb frowned. Wyatt laughed. The
other horses whispered.
"Stop!" called Twinkle.

Sasha knew she was in big trouble, but she couldn't make herself stop. Her hooves left the ground. She leaped high over the big, flat rock. A soft wind blew through her mane. The wind grew stronger. It swirled around her. It pulled her up toward the clouds.

What's happening? Sasha wondered as she squeezed her eyes shut.

Bam! Her hooves landed back on the ground.

CHAPTER 5) Sparkle!

Sasha opened her eyes. She trotted, kicking up some dirt. Then she slowed. Her heart raced from leaping.

"Sasha!" Caleb scolded. "What was that?"

Everyone in the class watched as Caleb slowly walked over to her. Sasha gulped. *Here comes trouble,* she thought.

"I'm so sorry. I didn't mean to jump," said Sasha.

"Those are your legs, right?" asked Caleb. "Your brain tells your legs what to do."

"It didn't feel that way." Sasha tried to explain. "I got this feeling . . . this itching that started on my back . . . and then I just had to jump."

Caleb widened his eyes.

"Yeah, right!" Chester laughed. He didn't believe her. No one did.

Sasha wished she were better at explaining. How could she say that she'd felt as if the clouds were calling to her? That sounded so . . . silly.

"You didn't follow my directions, Sasha," said Caleb. "You get a zero today."

Twinkle gasped. "Me too?"

"Please! It's not Twinkle's fault," Sasha told Caleb. "She should get a good grade. She's great at walking in line."

"You're right. Only you will get the bad grade," said Caleb.

Sasha turned to Twinkle to say she was sorry for being a bad partner, but Twinkle turned away. "Class is over," said Caleb.

Twinkle hurried off before Sasha could stop her. Chester and the other horses hurried off too. Only Wyatt and her sisters stayed.

"I thought you were funny, Sasha," said Wyatt.

Sasha hung her head. She hadn't wanted to be funny. She'd wanted to be a good partner. She wished she could have a do-over.

"Why couldn't you just stay in line like everyone else?" asked Zara.

"Sasha always has to be different," Poppy pointed out.

"It's better to be different than boring," said Wyatt.

"Humph!" said Poppy. She didn't believe Wyatt.

Sasha sighed. She didn't want to be boring, but she didn't want to get into trouble, either.

Just then Sasha heard a squawking sound. A group of ducks flew across the sky. The ducks flew in the shape of a *V*. Sasha spotted an empty space in the *V*. She wished she could be up there too.

No! That's crazy, she told herself. *You're a horse—not a bird!*

"Sasha, look!" cried Zara. "You're sparkling!"

Sasha gasped. Silver sparkles crackled on her white patch.

"That's so cool!" cried Wyatt.

"Does it hurt?" asked Poppy.

"Not at all." Sasha couldn't stop staring. She *was* sparkling!

CHAPTER 6) The Big Secret

Her patch quickly stopped sparkling. *Why did it do that?* Sasha wondered.

She hurried to find her mom at the stream. The stream flowed down from the mountains. Cool water bubbled over the rocks. Sasha's mom took a drink.

Her dad talked nearby with Wyatt's mom. All the families in the valley lived together in a group called a herd. Wyatt's mom was the head of their herd. Sasha's dad's job was to find the best grass for the herd to eat.

"What's wrong, sweetie?" Sasha's mom gave her a gentle nuzzle. Her mom always knew when she was sad or confused.

"I'm not like the other horses here," said Sasha.

"That's a great thing. You have a spark," said her mom.

Sasha jolted. "What?" *Does she know?* she wondered.

"A spark means you have much more energy." Her mom grinned. "You're my little firecracker."

Sasha liked when her mom called her that. Her mom didn't know, after all. Sasha took a deep breath. "No one else has a white patch like mine."

"Your cloud," said her mom.

"My cloud?" asked Sasha.

"I've always thought your patch looked like a fluffy, white cloud," said her mom.

Sasha twisted her neck. Her mom was right. It really did look as if she were carrying a cloud on her back!

"Why am I the only one who has it?" asked Sasha.

"You're special," her mom said. "You should be proud."

"I know that other horses have markings, like how Dad has white socks on his legs," said Sasha. "But my patch is different. My patch was sparkling today!"

"Sparkling?" cried her mom.

Sasha's dad's ears perked up. He left Wyatt's mom and hurried over.

"It was sparkling," her mom told him quietly.

"It is time to tell her our secret," whispered her dad.

"Now?" asked her mom. "Are you sure?"

"Yes. She is old enough," whispered her dad.

"Old enough for what? What secret?" asked Sasha.

"*Shh!*" said her parents. They nodded toward Wyatt's mom, still nearby. They didn't want her to hear.

Sasha couldn't believe it. Her parents had a secret—and it was about her!

CHAPTER 7

The Story of Sasha

"What secret?" Sasha asked her parents again.

They had walked to a small waterfall at the far end of the stream. The rush of water blocked their voices. No one could listen now.

"You were not born in Verdant Valley like all the other horses in our herd," began her mom.

"Oh." Sasha had thought the secret would be a lot more exciting. "Where was I born?"

Sasha had heard there were different valleys. Maybe she had been born in one of them.

"We don't know," said her dad. "You were a gift."

"A gift?" Sasha giggled. "Like a present with wrapping paper and a bow?"

"Sort of," said her mom.

"That's why you're so special," said her dad.

Sasha was confused. "I don't get it."

"Follow me," said her dad. "I'll show you."

Sasha's dad led them across the valley. He stopped at the bottom of Mystic Mountain, which was the tallest mountain. Its peak reached high into the clouds.

"I'll tell you the story of baby Sasha," he said.

Sasha swallowed hard. She was excited and nervous at the same time.

"One night there was a huge storm," he began. "The sky was dark. Rain poured down. Thunder boomed."

"We huddled here to stay dry." Her mom pointed to a nook in the side of the mountain. A rock jutted out to make a roof. "We had Zara and Poppy with us. They were just babies."

"Then the biggest bolt of lightning cut through the sky. We had never seen lightning like this. It turned the sky into a rainbow of sparkling colors," said her dad.

"A minute later, we heard a cry," said her mom. "We hurried out into the rain."

"A newborn foal was wrapped in a golden blanket," said her dad. "She was beautiful. And she had a white patch on her back."

"And for a moment, the patch sparkled," added her mom.

"Was that me?" asked Sasha.

"That was you," they both said.

"But where did I come from?" Sasha looked up at the tall mountain.

"We don't know. We searched and searched in the storm. There were no other horses around," said her mom. "It was a mystery."

"There was a note on your blanket." Her dad walked to a small pile of rocks. "We saved it."

He pushed the rocks aside. A piece of paper lay underneath. It was dirty, but they could still see the words.

Sasha read the note aloud.

Please keep Sasha safe until we can see her again.

She had so many questions. They swirled in her head. "Who left me here? When are they coming back?" she asked.

Her mom and dad didn't know. They had taken Sasha in and cared for her as their own daughter. They told everyone that she was found all alone in the storm.

"We didn't tell anyone about the strange lightning or your golden blanket with the note," said her dad. "Not even Zara and Poppy."

"You are part of our family. We will always love you. We will always keep you safe." Her mom pulled Sasha close.

"The secret is yours now," said her dad. "You can tell or not tell. It's up to you."

Sasha didn't want Zara and Poppy to know how different she really was. "I'm going to keep it secret," she said.

CHAPTER 8) Up to the Top

"Sasha, you're not even trying!" Wyatt called out the next morning.

They were playing Catch-the-Tail. It was her favorite game. Wyatt stood right behind her. She could have easily reached out and grabbed his tail—but she didn't. She was staring up at Mystic Mountain.

Did I come from up there? she wondered.

"Let's go up the mountain," she told Wyatt.

"Why?" asked Wyatt. They had never gone up the mountain before.

"Because—" Sasha almost blurted out her secret. "Because there are wildflowers at the top to eat," she said instead.

"Let's go." Wyatt never turned down food.

They began to climb. The path was rocky.

"Did you ask your mom about the sparkling?" asked Wyatt.

"She told me—oops!" Sasha pressed her lips closed. "I can't tell you."

"Why not?" he asked.

"It's a secret," said Sasha.

"I love secrets!" cried Wyatt. "Give me a hint."

"No way." Sasha was bursting to tell him, but she was worried he wouldn't be able to keep her secret. "Let's play Follow-the-Leader. I'll be the leader." Sasha hoped a game would take Wyatt's mind off of her secret.

Sasha ate a leaf from a low-hanging branch. Wyatt ate a leaf too.

"Come on. Tell me the secret," said Wyatt.

Sasha kept her lips zipped.

She flicked her tail to greet a mountain goat. Wyatt flicked his tail too.

They climbed higher and higher. The path snaked around the mountain.

Sasha crushed red berries with her hoof. She smeared them to draw a big S.

"Your turn," she told Wyatt.

Wyatt drew a W with his crushed berries.

"Hey! The leader drew an S," Sasha pointed out.

"W is for Wyatt," said Wyatt, "but S is for secret. I'll draw an S if you tell me the secret."

"I can't, Wyatt," Sasha said.

Wyatt bent down to bite a purple flower. "These flowers are yummy."

"Don't eat them," said Sasha.

"Why not? You said we were looking for flowers, and I'm hungry," Wyatt said.

"We need to go to the top of the mountain," she said. "There will be better flowers there." She began to climb.

Wyatt snorted and climbed after her. "I know your secret," called Wyatt.

Oh no! she thought. "You do?" she asked.

"You're bossy." He laughed. Sasha tried to laugh too, but her white patch had started to itch. What did that mean? Was something going to happen?

"I'm the leader now." Wyatt walked in front. "Follow me!"

He hurried around a path. Sasha followed. She peeked over the edge of the mountain. Their herd looked like tiny dots in the field below. The ground was a long way down.

Wyatt jumped over a bush.

Sasha jumped, but her jump was too big. *"Aaahhhh!"* Sasha tumbled through the air. She had jumped right off the mountain!

Wind rushed at her. Sasha's body spun around, making her dizzy. And then she stopped spinning. Sasha looked down. The ground was still far below. She passed over the stream and then over the waterfall.

Whoa! I'm moving, she thought. *But how?*

Sasha turned her head and gasped. Two huge wings had sprouted from the patch of white on her back. "I'm flying!" cried Sasha.

Sasha flew through the air. The feathers in her wings sparkled in the sun. Her mane glittered.

At first she didn't know how to steer. She flew in a crazy zigzag across the sky. She was scared.

Then Sasha flapped her
wings. She used the wind to
push her forward. She began to
fly smoothly. She flew fast. She
flew slow. She did a fancy loop
the loop. Rainbows exploded
from her tail.

Sasha giggled. Flying was
more fun than galloping!
Flying was amazing!

She circled back to Mystic Mountain and landed at the very top. She looked around. The only one here was a goat. He was surprised to see a flying horse!

Sasha twisted to look at her wings.
They were gone!

Sasha puzzled over this. What made
her wings come, and what made them
go away?

"Sasha!" Wyatt called. He was looking
for her.

Sasha's stomach twisted. She had forgotten all about Wyatt while she was flying. Wyatt was her better-than-best friend. He never cared that she was different from the other horses—but wings and flying were *very, very* different.

Maybe he didn't see me fly, Sasha thought.

"There you are!" Wyatt hurried up to her.

"Hi!" Sasha tried to act as if nothing had happened. "What's up?"

"What's up?" cried Wyatt. "*You* were up! I saw you. You can fly!"

Sasha held her breath. She was scared. Would he make fun of her? Would he not want to be her friend? "What do you think?" she asked.

"I think it's amazing!" cried Wyatt. "You can go anywhere!"

"You're right!" Sasha nodded at the forest of tall trees. "I can fly beyond the trees now."

"Will you go explore?" asked Wyatt.

"For sure." Sasha looked out at the big blue sky. She had always wanted to explore. "But, Wyatt, do you promise not to tell anyone?"

"You can trust me!" Wyatt said.

Sasha relaxed a little. "I wonder if there are other horses like me out there," she said. "Horses that can fly."

Suddenly, she knew what she would do. Sasha smiled. "I'm going to find them."

Read on for a sneak peek
from the second book in the
Tales of Sasha series!

CHAPTER 1) Show Me Your Wings

"Guess what!" cried Sasha.

Her hooves kicked up clumps of grass as she trotted across the field. She stopped in front of her two sisters, Zara and Poppy. They stood in the shade of the big cottonwood tree.

"Guess what!" she cried again. Sasha was terrible at keeping secrets.

Zara didn't answer. She was busy. "Away . . . play . . . say . . . " she said quietly. She was writing a poem. She needed the perfect rhyming word.

Poppy didn't answer. She was busy too. Poppy swatted flies with her tail. The flies flew around the flowers in her long mane.

Sasha let out a whinny. She hated when her sisters didn't listen to her.

Zara was the oldest sister. She had a jet-black coat and a chestnut brown mane and tail. Poppy was the middle sister. She had a chestnut brown coat and a jet-black mane and tail. Sasha was the youngest sister. She was all gray, except for a white patch on her back. She always felt like the plain sister, but not today.

Today, Sasha felt superspecial, and she had to tell her sisters why. Her secret was too exciting to keep to herself. "I have wings!" cried Sasha.

That did it. Zara spoke up. "You don't have wings. You're a horse, not a bird."

"I'm a horse with wings," said Sasha.

Poppy laughed. "Is this a game?"

"No! This is real," said Sasha. "Yesterday, Wyatt and I hiked to the top of Mystic Mountain."

"Why did you and Wyatt go up

there?" asked Zara.

"We went to eat wildflowers," said Sasha, "but I fell off the mountain!" Sasha shivered, remembering how scared she'd felt. "Wings popped out from the white patch on my back. Real wings!" cried Sasha. "I flew around and around."

Zara snorted. "You're making that up. Where are they now?"

"I'm telling the truth," said Sasha. "My wings went away after I flew back to the mountain."

"I want to see them," said Poppy. "Show us your wings."

Sasha had always known she was different from the horses in their valley. She dreamed of visiting far-off places. She ran the fastest and jumped the highest. Now she was different in the most amazing way. She had wings!

Sasha walked into the open field. She

watched the birds flutter in the sky.

Come out, wings, she thought.

She waited.

"Wings, wings, wings," she repeated.

Nothing happened.

Maybe I need to move, she thought. Sasha began to trot.

No wings came out.

She looked over at her sisters. Zara listed more rhyming words. "Stay . . . way . . ." Poppy swatted a fly with her tail. They didn't believe she had wings.

She had to show them! She ran faster.

Still no wings.

Suddenly, she had the worst thought. *What if my wings never come out again?*

Sasha picked up speed. She galloped past Caleb, her teacher at school. Sasha couldn't slow down to say hello.

She raced past a group of trees. She spotted a large branch on the ground, and her white patch began to itch. She knew this feeling. Her white patch itched when her body wanted to jump. Her legs sprang off the ground. A cool breeze flowed through her mane as she soared high over the branch.

Sasha didn't come back down.

She looked to the left and saw clouds. She looked to the right and saw birds. She looked at her back—and saw two beautiful wings!

"She's flying!" her sisters cried from down below. "Sasha can really fly!"

Alexa Pearl is the author of more than forty children's books. She lives in New Jersey with her family.

Paco Sordo is a comics artist, animator, and illustrator based in Spain. Visit him online at pacosordo.com.